Sweet Tooth

Laura Nyman Montenegro

With Much Love,
Laura Nyman Montenegro

Houghton Mifflin Company
Boston 1995

For Michael

Library of Congress Cataloging-in-Publication Data

Montenegro, Laura Nyman.
  Sweet Tooth / by Laura Nyman Montenegro.
  p.   cm.
  Summary: A girl is separated from her beloved lion because of ignorance and prejudice.
  ISBN 0-395-68078-6
  [1. Lions—Fiction.   2. Circus—Fiction.]   I. Title.
PZ7.M7635Sw   1995   93-49643
[E]—dc20   CIP
                           AC

Printed in the United States of America

BVG   10   9   8   7   6   5   4   3   2   1

We were clowns, my father and I, in our own family circus.

We would tumble and dance and pound on the drum amidst roars of laughter. And though the crowds clapped wildly for us, what they loved most was when I beat the drum and we pulled back the curtain for Sweet Tooth, my most beautiful lion.

Where we traveled no one had ever seen a lion, and he brought us great success. But our good fortune was not to last for long. Our troubles began one summer evening, when Sweet Tooth wandered into town in search of something sweet. There he peeked into the house of old Mrs. Stickpins.

She was a keeper of birds. Hundreds of birds. When her birds saw Sweet Tooth, they flew straight into the treetops. And Sweet Tooth, frightened by their squawking, trampled her petunias. Old Mrs. Stickpins threatened to have us all run out of town.

The acrobat came to my father and said, "I knew that lion would get us into trouble." But my father knew how much I loved Sweet Tooth and he convinced the acrobat to give my lion another chance.

I tried to keep a close eye on Sweet Tooth after that. But one night in autumn we were called away from our supper to watch a rainstorm and Sweet Tooth stole the ballerina's birthday cake from off the table.

Everyone was angry. I begged them all to realize that Sweet
Tooth was wild but noble and loyal and that he meant no real
harm. We all sat down and finished our meager meal in silence.

Sweet Tooth tried to be extra good after that. If the acrobat's hat blew off, he fetched it.

If the ballerina's feet hurt, he gave her a ride to lunch.

But a few weeks later, in a cold music hall, we began our show for a sparse and impatient crowd. A boy slipped his hand from his mother's grip and wandered backstage. There he pulled Sweet Tooth's tail. Sweet Tooth was startled. He let out a roar. The juggler dropped his plates.

"You vagabonds!" the boy's mother yelled. "My baby was nearly eaten by that beast!" As she stood there scolding me, I began to cry. I knew that my days with Sweet Tooth had come to an end.

    I lay in my trailer that night and peered out the window through the gently falling snow. I saw my father approaching. As he stepped in and shook the snow off his coat, I knew what he was going to say, so I said it for him. "I'll go say goodbye to Sweet Tooth."

We trudged through the snow to Sweet Tooth's wagon. Two men were easing his cage onto a waiting train. Sweet Tooth lay with his head on his paws, as if he knew he had done something wrong. "Sweet Tooth," I said, "you are good. Very, very good." I said goodbye as they slid the big door shut.

Late into the night I lay awake staring at the rounded
ceiling of my metal wagon.

I could not help but hear the high, thin whistle of a
train far, far away.

Our circus went on, but with Sweet Tooth gone there was something missing. I could no longer beat my drum with feeling. Our hearts were not in it, and the audience knew. My father and I sold the circus and finished out the winter sleeping on the cold, cold ground.

Then one day in early spring, my father and I found ourselves standing before an enormous circus tent. As we passed the animal cages, I saw the shadow of a lion cast upon a ragged canvas screen.

"Add bigger claws to his feet," a voice yelled from behind the curtain. "And polish his teeth. We want him to look ferocious!"

"Papa," I said, "wait!" But before I could see what was happening my father pulled me along to the ticket booth and bought two tickets.

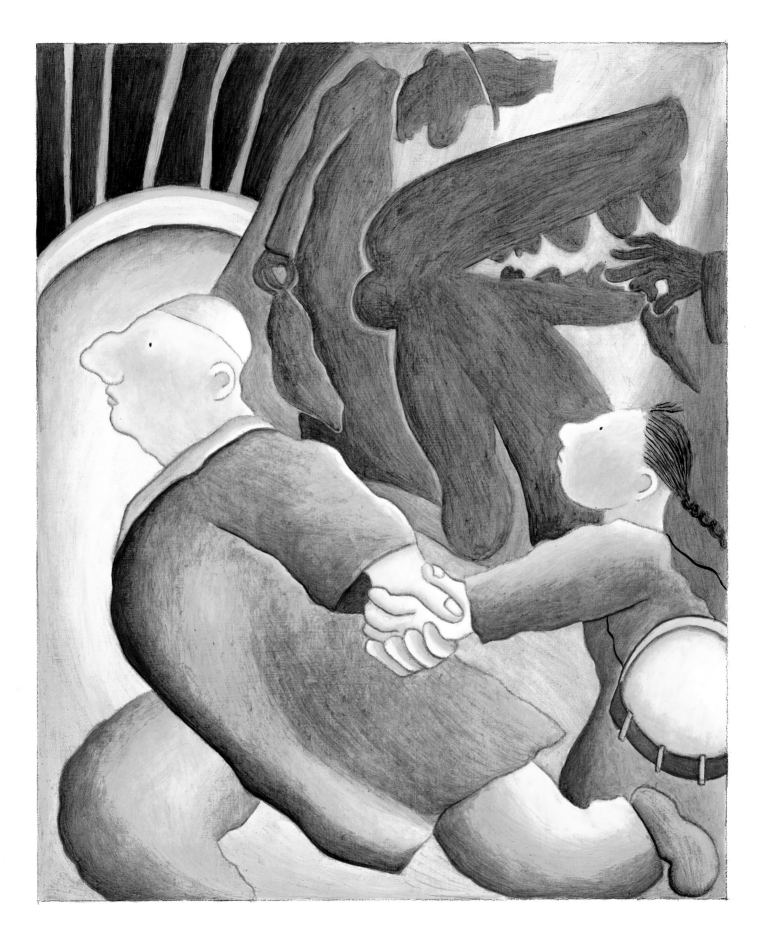

We were swept into the tent and up a narrow stairway to our seats. The lights swirled colors around and around and men on stilts came and went, throwing buckets of colored paper and balloons. Arabian horses covered with ribbons spun around the ring, and Russian tumblers did somersaults off the horses' backs.

Suddenly there was a hush and a pounding of drums and all went dark. A booming voice echoed throughout the tent. "And now! To top off this magical feast, we present with pleasure A FORMIDABLE BEAST!"

A woman in diamonds blew a whistle. The lion was led
out from the side of the tent and prodded up on a stool. The
ringmaster held out a hoop. A whip cracked. The drum rolled.
But nothing happened. The audience waited, the band waited

. . . all was silent.

Then suddenly from the depths of the lion's soul rose the angriest roar, a roar that shook the tent and rattled the drums and blew the hats off the people's heads.

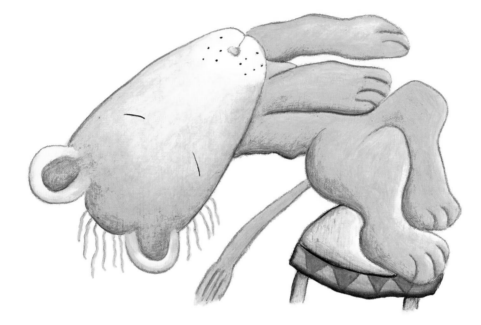

And then the lion, his eyes shut tight, fell to the floor. The ringmaster threw down his hoop. The shocked audience filed out.

We sat silently together, my father and I. Down on the stage lay our beautiful lion, Sweet Tooth. We rose and walked slowly down the aisle and knelt by his side. Out of the stillness I heard my own voice cry out, "Is he dead?"

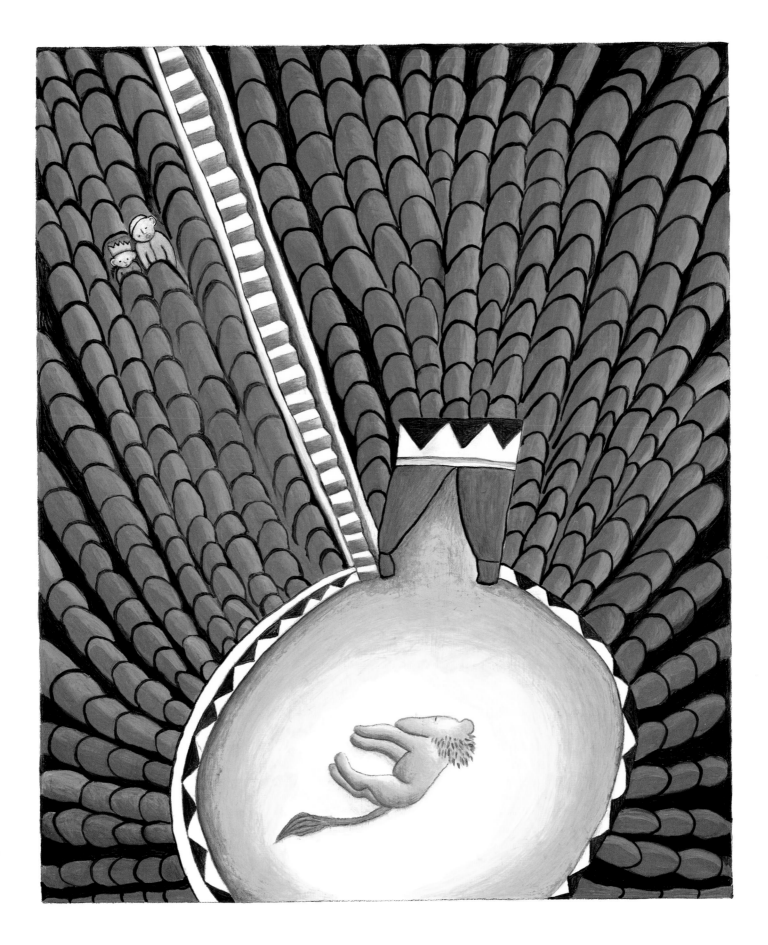

I placed my ear upon Sweet Tooth's side and heard there a pounding heart. It reminded me of a circus drum, pounding and pounding. I closed my eyes and I could see us as we had been, dancing and tumbling beneath the summer trees.

I picked up my drum and beat it, loud, and Sweet Tooth, as if waking from a dream, opened his eyes to look at me. I knew, at that moment, that we would gather our friends, our costumes and horns, and I would again beat the drum for my beautiful lion, Sweet Tooth.

And that is exactly what we did.